SABLE

SABLE

KAREN HESSE

Illustrated by Marcia Sewall

SCHOLASTIC INC.
New York Toronto London Auckland Sydney

ISBN 0-590-61967-5

Text copyright © 1994 by Karen Hesse. Illustrations copyright © 1994 by Marcia Sewall. All rights reserved. Published by Scholastic Inc., 555 Broadway, New York, NY 10012, by arrangement with Henry Holt and Company, Inc.

20 19 18 17 16   0/0

Printed in the U.S.A.   23

First Scholastic printing, September 1995

Contents

1 / The Arrival

Mam would not hear about having a dog. She didn't like them, none of them. She didn't even like Mr. and Mrs. Cobb's old hound, Truman. And Truman was as easygoing as a flat tire.

I had no hope of getting a dog when Sable wandered down off the mountain last October. The maples had turned flame red, and that morning, frost glittered on the windshield of Pap's pickup.

Eden, Mam's crimp-tailed cat, saw the dog first. She arched her back and hissed at the porch door.

"What is it?" Mam asked. Mam stood tall at the sink, toes turned out, looking over her shoulder.

Eden growled in her gray, silk throat. She flattened her ears.

"There's a dog out here, Mam!" I said, pressing against the storm door.

"Get your hand off that latch, Tate Marshall," Mam ordered.

She marched across the kitchen toward me, wiping her hands on her apron, and peered out the back door.

Eden was all riled up, hissing and growling and looking three times her size, while the dog just sat, drooping on the back porch. Bones held together by a dark brown coat, that's all she was. The longer she sat, the more she sagged, till her nose nearly touched the porch floor.

"Poor dog," I whispered, touching my fingers to the glass.

The dog looked up—not at me exactly; not at Mam, either. She stared at nothing in particular.

Just moved her head in the direction of the kitchen door.

Her stirring scared Eden half to death. Mam's cat slipped like gray smoke behind the fridge.

The dog staggered to her feet and wobbled a step or two away from us. Then she stopped. She leaned against the porch rail, panting.

"She looks awful thirsty, Mam," I said. "Should I put some water out for her?"

Mam's face tightened a bit, but then she nodded. "I guess some water would be okay," she said. "Just push the bowl out the door, Tate. Don't you go out there yourself. There's no trusting a stray."

"Yes, ma'am," I said, filling a small mixing bowl with cool water. "Should I feed her something, too?"

"Not a bite, Tate," Mam said. "Don't even think about giving that dog a reason for staying."

I slid the bowl out the door, slopping water over the cuff of my shirt. The dog inched up slowly, sniffing, and started to drink.

Just then, Pap came out of his shop, heading toward the house for his morning snack. He was wearing his blue Saxonville baseball cap.

Before he covered half the distance between the shop and the kitchen, he spotted the dog on the porch. Pap's face shifted into a question. The dog wagged her tail weakly.

"Poor thing," Pap said, coming up and fitting his hand over the bones of the dog's head. "Where'd you come from?"

I called from inside the kitchen, "She just showed up, Pap. She won't bite, will she? Mam thought she would, but I don't. I think we should feed her."

Mam looked up from the sink and scowled.

The storm door banged shut as Pap came into the kitchen. Scrambling down the porch steps, the dog fled, tail between her legs. She crept back up, though, a few seconds later, and finished emptying the water from the mixing bowl.

Pap slipped one of Mam's biscuits soaked in milk gravy to me.

"Ransom!" Mam said, frowning.

"The dog's near starved," Pap answered.

I took the biscuit from Pap and followed him out of the kitchen onto the porch, cushioning the storm door behind me.

Easing down, I held the biscuit on my open palm. Cautiously, the dog came over, her nose stretched way out in front of her, sniffing. The closer she got, the faster my heart beat.

Finally she came close enough to take the biscuit from my hand, real easy. She swallowed it without chewing.

After she'd finished licking her whiskers real good, she sniffed the gravy streaks on my fingers. Then she made a start of cleaning me.

I guess I grinned wider than a half moon, feeling that tongue wipe across my palm.

She was all the dog I ever wanted, dark brown except for a blaze of white on her chest and the tip of her tail. Even with brambles stuck in her dusty fur, there had never been a more perfect dog.

My hand stroked her bone-hard head and down

her ears. Those ears—that dog had the softest ears. They reminded me of the trim on the sweater Pap got for Mam one year. Pap said the trim was a kind of fur called sable.

"Come on, Sable," I said, coaxing her down off the porch.

"Named her, have you?" Pap said.

"Yes, sir," I answered.

2 / A Collar for Sable

Except for her being so skinny, Sable unfolded into a good-sized dog. She leaned against me, standing in the doorway to Pap's shop.

"If you're coming in, get on with it, Tate," Pap said. "You're letting the heat out."

I nudged Sable inside, shutting the door behind me.

Pap builds furniture for people who live in places like Boston and Hartford.

I wished Pap would let me work along with him.

He never did. Pap said, "Ten is too young to work with saws and things. Besides, girls have plenty other jobs to do without messing with wood." My stomach always tightened when Pap said stuff like that.

I knelt beside Sable, stroking her all over, getting to know her with my hands. "How come Mam doesn't like dogs?" I asked.

Pap shrugged. He held a pencil between his teeth as he sighted down a piece of white oak.

Pap made a mark on the wood with the pencil. "Mam got herself tore up by a dog when she was a girl," he said. "You've seen that scar on her leg, Tate."

"I didn't know that was from a dog," I said. Mam always wore dresses that hid the scar. She didn't even like me seeing it.

The shop smell tingled inside my nose, like a sneeze coming. I wiggled my nostrils in and out, trying to get the tickle to settle down.

"She was younger than you when it happened,"

Pap said. "We'd have had a dog a long time ago if it was up to me. I always had dogs when I was growing up. Your great-grandmam raised them."

"She did?" I asked.

"Beauties," Pap said. "Elkhounds."

My hand rested on Sable's head. "Do you think we could raise Sable?"

A knot tightened right inside my throat, waiting for Pap's answer.

"Even if Mam was willing," Pap said, "that mongrel's sure to disappear in a day or two. Just passing through—that's my bet. Don't get attached to it, Tate."

"No, sir," I said, chewing on my lip.

Pap switched on the planer and started running the oak through. Sable tucked her tail between her legs and backed toward the door.

"Come on, girl," I said, leading her out of Pap's shop. "You don't have to stay in here if you don't want."

Sable and I walked the property line, from Mam's willow in front to the sour apple out back. Plucking a stunted apple from the sour tree, I took a bite, puckered, and offered Sable the rest. Sable ate that sour apple, core and all.

"Sable," I said. "I've got someplace I want to show you."

We crossed the yard and climbed the path into the woods. Following the trail, we entered a small clearing surrounded by maple and pine trees.

"Used to be someone had a cabin up here," I told Sable. "A long time ago, before the river changed course."

In the center of the clearing stood a stone foundation and the remnants of a chimney.

"This is my secret place," I told Sable. "I have it fixed up just right with everything I need."

I stashed my best stuff up there: my rock collection, my treasure box. Tucked it all on a shelf inside the old fireplace. I had a pocketknife and soap for whittling, all kinds of string, a family of spool dolls.

Digging around in the treasure box, I uncovered a ball of twine.

"How about I make you a collar, Sable?" I asked. "Think you'd like that?"

Sable sniffed the twine in my hands, then lay down in the leaves at my feet.

I measured and cut three long strands and started braiding them. Holding the plaited twine against Sable's neck every now and then, I tested until I had a piece long enough. Sable sat patiently as I tightened the ends around her neck into a square knot.

Next, I pulled out my old hairbrush and plucked the bristles clean. Sable sniffed the honey-colored cloud of my hair. She tried eating it.

"Don't eat that, Sable!" I cried. "It'll make you sick."

I blew the hair cloud away, into the chilly afternoon. "Maybe some mouse will use it," I said. "To make a nest."

Gently, I dragged my hairbrush through Sable's matted fur, careful not to pull. I worked at her tangles, the way Pap worked at mine, until I'd eased them all out.

"You sure look pretty, Sable," I said when I finished. Sable wagged her tail in a tired circle. All groomed, with a collar on, she really looked like she belonged to somebody.

In the worst way, I wanted her to belong to me. But where could I keep her? Mam wouldn't let her in the house, not if she was scared of dogs.

And I couldn't leave her outside, what with the nights so cold and Sable so weak and skinny. And what if she ran away?

I decided I'd build a doghouse. If Pap would let me.

3/The Bed

"Pap?" I called, poking my head inside the shop. Pap stood at his bench, gluing up boards. "Pap, can I use some of your wood to build a house for Sable?"

"Sorry, Tate," Pap said, shaking his head. "This wood's too good for any doghouse."

I guess I knew he wouldn't let me. About all Pap ever lets me use are his stickers. Those are the strips he puts between planks when he's drying wood. He's got a lot of stickers, but I couldn't figure how to build a doghouse out of them.

"Come on, girl," I called to Sable.

We hunted in the shed behind Pap's shop. Dress-ers, and bed frames, and boxes of canning jars leaned against the rough pine walls. I swiped at spiderwebs. "There must be something in here we can use for you," I told Sable.

She turned her head in my direction. I wiped my dusty hands on the seat of my pants and stooped down. Holding Sable's brown jaw in one hand, I stroked the top of her bony head with the other. She still wouldn't look right at me.

"I'll figure out something for you, girl," I whis-pered. "Don't worry."

I'd hoped to find a big empty carton I could maybe cut a door into. Or a wooden crate. All I found was a worn-out cardboard box; it didn't even have the flaps that make the top.

"Well, this will have to do," I said. "It'll make a good bed at least, Sable. Hold on. I'll clean it up for you."

I knocked the dried leaves and dead bugs out of

the corners. Then I turned the box upside down and banged on the bottom, raising a puff of dust.

Sable sneezed. I sneezed, too.

"We need something soft to put in here, don't we, girl?" I asked. "It's not really a bed until it's soft."

I thought Pap's sawdust might work as bedding. I led Sable back around to the shop.

Pap's piles of sawdust were stacked up like fine raked leaves. I wished I could jump in those piles, but Pap's broom was always leaning over them, just daring me to try.

"What you doing out there in the shed, Tate?" Pap asked.

"Just looking around," I said.

"Don't be making a mess, girl," Pap warned.

"No, sir."

I stood, staring at Pap's back. His dark hair poked through the hole above the plastic snaps in his baseball cap.

"Pap, can I use some of your sawdust?" I asked.

Pap nodded, not even looking over at me. "Just don't trail it across the floor," he said. "And shut that door behind you, Tate."

I closed the door and knelt in front of the tallest pile. Using my hands, I scooped sawdust into Sable's box. Sable pushed her nose into the middle of things, helping.

"Okay, girl," I said, standing up and brushing dust off my knees. The sawdust reached about half-way up the box sides. "Come on. Try it out."

I pushed the box right in front of her.

Sable stared at me. Then she stared at the box. Instead of climbing in, she walked right past it, plopping down on the hard shop floor.

"Not there, Sable," I said. "In your bed."

Sable dragged herself up onto her feet again. She had sawdust all over her newly brushed fur.

"I should put something on top of the sawdust, shouldn't I, Sable?"

I remembered the old stained quilt from Grandmam Betts. It wasn't nice enough to put on a bed anymore. But it would do all right for Sable.

"Can Sable stay in here a few minutes?" I asked Pap.

Pap nodded, too busy working to notice what I was up to.

"Okay, girl," I said. "Stay right here."

Sable sank to the floor again, sweeping sawdust with her tail as I backed out of the shop.

I climbed silently onto the back porch. Mam stood in the kitchen, listening to the radio, her sleeves pushed up past her elbows. The muscles worked in her long back as her fist kneaded dough.

Slipping around to the front of the house, past Mam's willow, I let myself in quietly. I crept up the stairs, careful to skip the creakers. My heart hammered against my throat. Mam would sure explode if she caught me giving Sable one of Grandmam Betts's quilts, even a ruined one. I managed to get the quilt down from the closet and out of the house without Mam knowing.

Pap looked up as I rushed through the shop door. My hair crackled, full of static from carrying the quilt on my head.

"Does Mam know you have that blanket?" Pap asked.

"No, sir," I said.

Pap nodded. "She's not going to like it."

"I didn't take a good quilt, Pap," I said.

"She's still not going to like it."

I folded and refolded the blanket, till I got it just right in Sable's box. "Okay, girl," I said. "It's ready now. Hop in."

Sable backed away from the box, her tail between her legs. I climbed inside it myself, showing her what to do.

"This is your bed, Sable."

She just sniffed inside my ear.

Finally I gave up trying to coax her. I just picked her up and put her in. For such a big dog, Sable weighed about as much as an empty school bag.

She stood on the quilt for a few seconds, looking wobbly. Then she sniffed the fabric, pawed some wrinkles into it, circled, and dropped her bones down.

Sable sighed, real long, like wind down a chimney. She rested her head on the edge of the cardboard box.

"Can we keep Sable's bed in your shop tonight?" I asked Pap.

Pap looked over and frowned. "We don't even know if that dog's housebroken, Tate. If she messes anything—anything," he said, "you're responsible."

"Yes, sir," I said.

I explained to Sable how she was a guest in Pap's shop. "You better behave," I told her.

Cooking up a pan of mush for Sable's supper, I stirred a spoon of bacon fat in to improve the flavor.

Sable ate her mush out on the porch, licking the bowl over and over, chasing it around with her tongue, until finally I took it away. Then I led her back toward Pap's shop. She didn't wait to be invited. She headed right inside out of the shivery cold as soon as I opened the door and clicked on the light. She climbed straight into her box.

"Don't get comfortable yet," I said. "Remember, Sable, no messes in this shop."

I led her back outside, standing in the patch of light from Pap's shop window, hopping up and down to keep warm. Sable didn't make me wait in the cold for long.

"You're a good dog," I said, hugging her skinny brown neck.

Sable smelled like dried leaves, and dust, and pine trees. Her warm breath tickled inside my ear. I buried my face in her dark coat, breathing her in. Sable stood still, her tail swaying gently behind her.

"Into bed now," I said. I fingered those ears of hers one more time. The white tip of her tail twitched against the side of her box. There was no room in her bed for a full tail wag.

Holding her face between my hands, I concentrated on fixing everything about her in my mind.

"Sable," I whispered.

For the first time she looked straight at me. Her eyes shone like chocolate melting in the pan, all liquid and warm and sweet.

A bubble of something joyous lifted inside me.

"Don't get into trouble tonight, Sable," I said. "Promise."

And be here in the morning, I prayed as I turned out the light and shut the shop door behind me.

That night I stared across the starlit yard. There was a dog sleeping in a cardboard box in Pap's shop. A real dog. Tomorrow I'd bring money to school and scoot over to Tom's General Store. I'd buy real dog food for Sable. When I got home, I'd teach her to sit, and stay, and roll over.

Mam and Pap hadn't said I could keep her.

But they hadn't said I couldn't, either.

4/Sable's Bad Habit

The next morning I woke as the smell of perking coffee needled the house. Pap snored in the next room and Mam sang country in the shower. I pulled on my overalls and raced to the shop.

Sable met me at the door, wagging her tail and sniffing my hands. "Good girl," I said, checking for messes and not finding any. I hugged her and led her outside.

"Want some breakfast?" I asked.

Sable sat on the back porch in the frosty morning, watching me through the storm door while I soaked some bread in milk.

She bolted down the soggy bread and sat waiting for more.

How could I leave her and go off to school? I wouldn't mind staying home. But I knew Mam and Pap wouldn't let me. Sometimes Pap took me along when he delivered a job out of town. He'd let me skip school for that, but not for a dog.

I looked at Sable and considered tying her. If I tied her, she'd surely be waiting for me when I got home. But then I thought about Raye Cather's dogs. Those dogs lay in their own mess, day in, day out. I couldn't do that to Sable.

"Don't run off while I'm gone today," I told her as we walked down the drive to the bus stop. "I'll be back at three. I promise."

Sable wagged her tail in the crinkly leaves, looking right at me. "When I get home, Sable, I'll feed you dog food from a can, and I'll teach you to sit."

Sable already sat pretty well on her own, but only when *she* felt like sitting.

The bus screeched to a stop in front of the driveway. Sable sat, watching, as I climbed the steps.

"Got yourself a dog?" the driver asked.

"Yes, ma'am," I said.

I hurried down the aisle to the back of the bus so I could see Sable out the rear window. Just before we turned the bend in front of the Cobbs', Sable lay down in the dust of our driveway, resting her head on her paws.

I couldn't stay fixed on my schoolwork that day, wondering if I'd find her when I got home. During recess I worked it out with Tom. I'd dust and sweep the store in exchange for dog food. Now, at least, I'd be able to feed Sable.

On the way home I strained my neck, trying to see our driveway as we came around the corner. If hoping could make a thing happen, Sable would surely be there. And then she was there, waiting at the bus stop for me, just where I'd left her.

She waited for me that first day. And the second too. She waited the whole first week. She was always there, sitting in the middle of our driveway, watching the bus pull up, wagging her tail.

I almost stopped worrying about her running off

when one morning, after she'd been with us a few weeks, instead of lying down like she usually did, Sable started running after the bus, trying to catch up. I watched, helpless, from the rear window as she sprinted down the road. She stayed close behind us, too, until we turned onto Route 30 and picked up speed.

I never was the best student to begin with. But that day I couldn't keep my mind on anything, knowing she might get hit by a car. Or wander so far she couldn't find her way back.

When I got home that afternoon, Sable wasn't at the bus stop to meet me. The sky hung low over the valley, heavy with snow. She might die, lost outside in the harsh weather.

I searched for her in Pap's shop, and at the secret place. I searched along the road, and down the river. My voice nearly gave out from calling her.

She came home, finally, when she was good and ready, after I'd wound myself tighter than a rope swing. She showed up at dusk, wagging her tail in a big circle, carrying an old rubber boot between her teeth.

I told her "no" and threw the boot into the woods. She started chasing after it, but I called her back and fed her supper.

I'd hoped that would end her wandering, but it didn't. She kept it up almost every day, taking off for hours, dragging junk home with her when she returned.

Once she brought a frozen wedge of chocolate cake. With the big chunk hanging from her mouth, she pranced into the yard, leaving a trail of dog prints in the fresh snow.

At first I laughed, watching her with that huge piece of cake hanging from her face.

Then I saw Mam.

Mam yelled out the storm door at Sable, and Sable took off, heading up the path toward the secret place. I ran after her.

"Sable," I said. "You've got to stop this."

Sable bowed down on her front legs and dropped

the cake. She barked, her rear end wagging up high in the icy air. She wanted to play.

"No, Sable," I said.

I called her over to where I sat on the stone foundation, the cold stabbing up through my bottom. Sable trotted over and rested her head on my leg.

"Listen to me, Sable," I said, chewing on my lip. "Mam's not crazy about you to begin with. If you're not perfect, absolutely perfect, I don't know what she'll do." I ran my gloved hand over Sable's head and down her ears. "Sable, you've got to be good."

Sable's eyes searched my face. She panted softly.

"What's the matter, girl?" I asked. "Don't I feed you right? Don't I take good care of you?"

Sable wagged her tail so hard her whole back end wagged with it. She looked at me with those dark eyes, her fuzzy brows rippling.

She didn't mean any harm. All she was doing, really, was bringing us presents.

But Mam didn't see it that way.

When I came back to the house after putting

Sable in the shop for the night, Mam served up a lecture. She'd been simmering it all afternoon.

"I don't know why I let you keep that dog in the first place," she said. "She's nothing but trouble. Imagine, stealing good food."

I sat at the kitchen table, chasing a crumb around with my fingertip.

"If you can't break her stealing, Tate," Mam said, "she has to go."

"No!" I cried.

Pap said, "Why don't you tie her, Tate?"

"Pap! We can't tie her. Sable's not like Raye Cather's dogs."

"Then teach her to stay," Pap said.

All my spare time I worked with Sable. I filled my coat pockets with Mam's sparkle cookies. If Sable did good, she got a piece of cookie right then and there.

But it took a whole day teaching her to stay behind the house while I went around front. And she never really learned *that* right.

"Stay, Sable," I commanded, in a voice as firm as Mam's.

"Stay," I repeated, walking backward around the side of the house.

Sable would stay for a minute, maybe. Then, all of a sudden, she'd burst around the corner of the house. As soon as she caught sight of me, she started jumping and barking and wagging her tail. She snuffled inside my pockets.

"No treat, Sable!" I cried, refusing to give her a cookie. "It doesn't count unless you stay till you're called."

Sable cocked her head to one side, sort of smiling at me, green sparkles on her nose and crumbs in her whiskers.

"Oh, all right," I said, giving in and feeding her a cookie. "We'll try again tomorrow."

But I couldn't be with her all the time. I had homework and my chores. And then there was the dusting and stuff I did for Tom at the general store to pay Sable's keep.

I couldn't expect Mam to keep track of her. Sable

didn't scare Mam so much anymore. Mam just plain didn't like her. And she didn't like my working at the general store, either. She said, "You're up there cleaning for Tom, but you don't lift a finger to help me."

I don't know what Mam needed my help for. She did fine on her own. Besides, I didn't like Mam's work. I liked Pap's work.

I considered asking Pap if he'd watch Sable. But Pap was already doing plenty, just letting Sable stay in the shop with him at night. He had a ton of orders to fill over the winter. Long after I fell into bed, I would gaze across the yard at the shop window. Pap moved in and out of view, working late.

The light from Pap's window soothed the dark. It spilled, warm and bright, across the silent, snowy yard. I imagined Sable twitching in her box, dreaming her dog dreams. After a while, Pap's machines always sang me to sleep.

"I'm taking Sable up to the secret place," I told Mam after school one frigid day in February.

Mam said, "It's too cold out there today, Tate. I want you to stay in."

"I'm dressed warm," I said, stepping onto the porch.

I caught sight of a garden basket with a broken handle at the edge of the yard. It didn't belong to us. I moved it before Mam saw it, too.

The cold pinched my nose and made my eyes crinkle when I blinked. Before Sable, I *would* have stayed inside on a day like this, but I had too much fun outside with Sable to let a little cold stop me.

The thick layers of snow clothes slowed me down as I plowed my way through the newest drifts. Sable raced far ahead of me, then doubled back, spraying snow in my face as she slid to a stop.

She ran circles around me, barking so much the echo brought snow down off the pine trees. Sable chased the snow as it fell, barking like a hammer blow, making more snow come down.

"Sable," I said, "you make winter perfect."

Except when you disappear, I thought. And drag trash back from half the valley.

5 / Stop, Sable!

Mrs. Elliot from the board of selectmen phoned to say there'd been complaints about Sable.

"Who complained?" I asked.

"Doesn't matter," Mam snapped. "She's bothering folks. That's all you need to know."

"I want to know who complained!"

"You just cool off, Tate Marshall," Mam said.

"No, I won't!" I stomped out of the kitchen onto the porch. Sitting on the cold step, I nearly froze my backside. My feet cramped as the chill crept up through my boots.

Sable sat beside me, her brown fur warm in the sun.

I put my arm across her back and leaned into her side.

"What kind of neighbor complains about a dog?" I asked. "It's not like other dogs never come on our property. They get into the compost and dig up the garden. But we never complain."

Sable panted softly, staring off into the snowy woods.

Mam turned on the radio loud. Pots and pans clanked in the kitchen.

When Pap came in for a cup of coffee, Mam gave him an earful.

Pap listened, hardly saying a word. When Mam's storm had blown itself out, Pap left the kitchen, heading straight for the shed. He found a heavy chain, hanging against the back wall. Pap hooked one end of that chain to the side of the shop. He hooked the other end to Sable.

I couldn't look at her. Sable wasn't a dog you chained. Pap and Mam were treating her like Raye

Cather treated her dogs. Sable pleaded with me to set her loose. I didn't dare. When I left in the morning for school, she howled so pitiful, it made my teeth hurt.

By the end of the week, though, Sable figured out how to get loose all by herself. Once she discovered the trick of freeing herself from the chain, she wasted no time in finding trouble again.

The day Sable brought home a brand-new mat that people use to wipe their feet on, Mam blew.

"Get rid of that dog," she said.

"No!" I cried, wrapping my arms around Sable.

"It's too much, Tate," Pap said. He spoke so soft, I could hardly hear him. "We can't keep her anymore."

"I'll tie her up, Pap," I said. "I'll tie her up so good she'll never get loose."

"You know you won't," Pap said. "She needs someone with her all the time. She needs training. At the very least, she needs a good fence."

"*We* could build a fence, Pap. Together."

Mam shook her head. "I've put up with her long

enough, Tate. The dog's nothing but trouble. She's got to go."

"No, Mam! Pap! Please!"

Mam turned her tall back on me and picked up the phone, calling neighbors, trying to find out who the mat belonged to.

I ran with Sable up to the secret place, without a coat even. Sable sat close beside me.

"You've gotten yourself into hot water with Mam before," I told Sable. "It'll be all right. I'm sure it will." But my heart beat so hard, I could see it thumping through my overalls.

"Maybe Mam will forget about that mat after a while, Sable."

Sable pushed her nose down my neck.

"Anyway," I said. "That's what we'll hope for."

6 | A Trip

Two weeks later, Pap had cabinets to deliver to a doctor in Concord, New Hampshire. He said I could skip school and come along.

"Bring the dog, too, Tate," Pap said, loading cabinets into the truck.

"Sable's coming?" I asked. Sable never rode in Pap's truck.

"Yup," Pap said.

When I unchained her from the shop, Sable ran in giant figure eights, all around the yard. I had some work getting her into the cab. I had to grab her by her braided collar and sort of haul her on in. That square knot I had tied held tighter than a stuck lid.

It was April and large patches of snow still dotted our property, but the dirt roads were thawing and that meant mud.

Sable panted in the sun-steeped truck. I opened my window a bit and she pushed her nose out, sniffing the spicy air. Sable sat beside me in the cab, her two front paws pressing into my legs. She sure wasn't skinny anymore.

"Ouch, Sable," I said, pushing her off of me.

Sable brought her head back inside the truck. Her tongue wiped across my cheek, leaving a sloppy wet streak. She snuffled the inside of my ear.

"Good dog," I said, stroking the soft white blaze on her chest.

Pap installed the new cabinets for Doc Winston while Sable and I chased chipmunks and frogs on the doctor's property. It might have been mud season in Vermont, but at Doc Winston's, the forsythia bloomed and the green grass made a soft mat under my boots.

A stone wall, taller than I was, wrapped around Doc Winston's land. He had a pond stocked with goldfish, and gardens, and a forest of pine trees. Our place and most of Mr. Cobb's would fit inside Doc Winston's walls. He even had a scrolly gate at the end of his driveway.

Sable and I didn't have enough time to explore half of it before Pap had finished.

"That's a fine dog you have," Doc Winston said, admiring Sable as he walked out with Pap toward the truck. Sable shot across the grass, smooth and sleek, chasing a rabbit.

"She's good company, all right," Pap answered, squinting after her. "It's a shame we can't keep her."

"Oh?" Doc Winston asked.

"She wanders sometimes," Pap said.

Pap whistled and Sable stopped chasing the rabbit. She turned and thundered over, coming to sit on the grass between me and Pap, panting.

"Wanders?" Doc Winston asked. "Couldn't you put in a fence?"

I looked at Pap.

Pap shook his head. "A fence big enough for this dog? Yours would do fine, but you've seen her run, Doc. It wouldn't be fair, shutting a dog like this up in anything smaller . . ." Pap's voice trailed off. I'd watched Pap play cards with Mr. Cobb and all. Something about the way Pap talked to Doc Winston felt like cardplaying.

"I can see she'd work wonders keeping down the rabbit population. She any good as a watchdog?" Doc Winston asked.

"Sure is," Pap answered. "She knows how to keep her eye on things, doesn't she, Tate?"

I had a real uneasy feeling about what was happening here.

"Look, if you're really thinking about giving her up," Doc Winston said, "I might take her."

Something twisted inside me.

"Would you?" Pap asked.

"Pap!"

"Listen, Tate," Pap said. "We couldn't find a better home for her than here."

"I've been thinking about getting another dog. It's been years since we lost Damon," Doc Winston said.

Pap nodded.

"You wouldn't need to worry about her, Tate," Doc Winston told me. "And you could come back to visit her anytime."

Black specks floated in front of my eyes. Come back to visit her! She was my dog!

"What do you think, Sable?" Doc Winston asked, stooping down. "You want to stay? You'd have a good home here. Plenty room to run."

I turned and glared at Pap.

Sable sat panting softly in the green grass, surrounded by Doc Winston's land. She held her sleek brown head high, gazing into the distance.

"Good dog," Doc Winston said, running an admiring hand down her.

I couldn't watch anymore. I ran to Pap's truck and slammed myself inside.

Pap had planned on leaving Sable here all along.

Pap poked his head inside the truck cab. "Come say good-bye to her, Tate."

I bit my lip and swallowed. "No, sir," I said.

As we backed out of the driveway, Sable trotted along beside us. Her head tilted to one side as Doc Winston closed the gate, locking her in. When we disappeared around the corner, Sable started barking like crazy.

I squeezed against my side of the truck cab, digging my fingernails into my palms.

The muscles worked up and down in Pap's jaw, but he kept on driving.

7/The Empty Bed

I shut myself up in my room and wouldn't come out. Right about then I hated Mam and Pap. I really did.

"Why don't you see how Pap's doing in the shop?" Mam said, coming into my room that evening after supper, a supper I had refused to eat.

"I don't care to," I answered.

Mam looked like she wanted to argue, but then she changed her mind and went back to the kitchen.

Pap came in and asked if I'd like helping him on a project in the shop.

Pap's asking like that made me angrier than ever.

I turned my head to the wall. "You never asked me to help before."

Why did he have to ask now? Now, when he knew I wouldn't!

When I finally left my room for school on Monday morning, I found Sable's empty bed off in the corner of Pap's shop, on top of a tall pile of stickers. Grandmam's blanket, newly washed, hung on the line, drying. I lifted the box and carried it gently back to the shed, tucking it away where it would be safe.

That's when I decided. I could make a fence good as Doc Winston's.

That afternoon I sorted through Pap's stickers, picking out the best ones. It took ten trips, carrying all that wood behind the shop. Mam's cat watched from the back porch.

After busting open a couple garbage bags, I slithered around in the crawl space under the shed, spreading the bags out. That plastic would keep the damp earth from rotting the stickers till I was ready to use them.

With Sable gone, I didn't need money for food anymore, but I kept working at Tom's anyway, saving for a hammer, nails, a saw. I bought the saw first, using it to cut sharp points on the ends of the stickers.

By late May, I had the other things I needed too.

Dragging the sticks out from under the shed, I carried an armful at a time across the yard.

I dropped each load with a clatter near the path to the secret place.

"What are you up to, Tate?" Pap asked.

"I'm building a fence, sir," I said.

"What you building a fence in the middle of the yard for?" Pap asked.

" 'Cause we need one here," I said.

I started by laying long pieces of wood end to end on the ground until I had outlined a run big enough for Sable. Spreading the stickers out along the frame, I began hammering, two nails at the top of each stick. I bent plenty nails, but that was all right. Sometimes I missed the nail and hit the ground, or I'd hit the wood and mess up the row of stickers not yet nailed down. Sometimes I smashed my thumb.

But slowly, the sections came together. When I finished hammering the last one, they looked like big hair combs laying there.

Now I needed to stand the sections up and drive them into the ground.

I lifted the first piece and started pounding. Immediately, I hit rock.

Digging out smaller stones, I lugged them over to Pap's rock pile. But some were just too big to move. I shifted the fence sections instead, and tried again in softer ground till I got them standing.

With the last section though, I hit more than rock. I struck ledge.

"I'll just make the gate out of this piece," I decided, "where Sable can go in and out." With rope, I tied one end to a section I already had standing.

On the opposite end, I screwed in a hook and eye. It took some tinkering, but I made a gate out of it.

For days I worked, whipping those stickers into a fence. My hands filled with splinters and blisters. My thumbnail turned black. Every part of me ached.

But in the end, when I stepped back and looked, I'd done a good job. It had to be good. It was for Sable.

8/The Runaway

Pap and Mam planned a trip to Hartford to visit Aunt Aurelia. I wasn't going. Aunt Aurelia kept a stash of candy in her pantry. That part I liked. But she always made me sit on the itchy sofa with her and talk about school. And she kept the temperature in her house hotter than July.

I had other plans.

"I guess you're old enough to stay on your own for a while," Pap said.

I listened for the sound of the truck engine firing up. Seemed like it took Mam and Pap half the morning to leave. Finally I heard the crunch of gravel under tires. I saw the dust kicked up behind them as they turned onto the road.

Now it was my turn. I was going to Concord to get Sable.

I had been walking for fifteen minutes, maybe, when Elton Cobb pulled up alongside me.

"Where you heading, Tate Marshall?" Mr. Cobb asked.

"Clear to Concord," I said. "To fetch my dog."

"Your folks know about this?" Mr. Cobb asked.

"No, sir," I said.

"Get in, Tate," Mr. Cobb said.

He drove me back home.

"Where *are* your folks?" he asked when he pulled into the empty drive.

"Off to Hartford," I said. "Visiting family."

"You look like you mean to get back on the road as soon as I drive away, Tate."

"I do, sir."

"Look. I have business in Concord on Tuesday,"

Mr. Cobb said. "You get permission from your folks and I'll take you with me. We'll drop in on that dog of yours."

"Yes, sir!" I said.

I spent the rest of the day counting how many hours there were between now and Tuesday. I was going to Concord.

Mam and Pap pulled in a little after seven that night, hours later than I'd expected. I'd already done my chores and fed Eden. I wasn't hungry myself. My stomach kept fizzing up at the thought of bringing Sable home.

Mam and Pap sat at the kitchen table, looking exhausted.

"What took you so long?" I asked.

"Aunt Aurelia didn't recognize us," Pap explained. "She wouldn't let us in."

Pap cleaned his fingernails with the blade of his pocketknife as he spoke. "She thought Mam was from some agency," Pap said, grinning.

"I'm beat," Mam said, scowling at the stove.

I knew this wasn't the best time to be asking about Sable. I should have let them settle down. But I couldn't help myself.

"Could we bring Sable back now?" I asked.

Pap spread his hands out on the tablecloth and studied them, sighing.

"I built a fence, Pap."

"There's other things you could have done around here a lot more useful than that," Mam said.

Mam and I glared at each other.

Then she dragged herself out of her chair. "I'll fry up some eggs for supper."

I had to make Mam understand how important it was to me, bringing Sable back.

"You sit down, Mam," I ordered. "I'll cook dinner tonight."

Mam gave me a funny look, but she settled back into her seat.

I fried up potatoes and onions, eggs and ham.

Pap made soft noises as he ate, dipping his bread into a puddle of egg yolk.

"Thank you, Tate," Mam said, finishing the last

of the potatoes. She wiped her mouth with a nap-
kin. "That was real good."

"My fence is good, too," I said.

Pap sighed.

"Can I at least go down and visit her? Doc Winston said to come anytime."

They stared at me.

"Mr. Cobb will drive me. He said he'd drive me
on Tuesday if you gave permission."

Pap rested his hand over top of Mam's. She studied me a minute, then she nodded.

Pap sat back in his chair. I poured out two cups
of strong coffee, and set one down in front of each
of them.

9 | The Storm

I tested my fence once more before I headed over to Mr. Cobb's house.

The sun chinned itself over the mountain. The trees above the ridge swayed, a high wind tossing them, but it was windless and hot down in the valley. I sat on Mr. Cobb's porch steps, waiting.

The Cobbs' hound, Truman, sat on the steps beside me.

"Morning, Tate," Mrs. Cobb said, coming out onto the porch. Truman got up, tail wagging, and waddled over to her.

Mrs. Cobb had already set the coffee to perk on her woodstove. She had bacon sizzling in the pan. "You care for some breakfast?"

"No, ma'am," I said, watching Truman follow on her heels. "I'm just waiting on Mr. Cobb."

"You got directions to that doctor's house?" Mr. Cobb asked as we wove our way over the mountain and turned onto Route 9.

He drove real slow, slow enough I could have run alongside and got there faster. Mr. Cobb's driving nearly drove me crazy. I just wanted to get to Concord, to Sable.

"Yes, sir," I said, bringing out the paper Pap had sketched a map on last night. I smoothed the directions out on Mr. Cobb's dashboard.

"I don't like the look of that sky," Mr. Cobb said. "See if you can tune in some weather, Tate."

I fiddled with Mr. Cobb's radio. I couldn't get much more than static.

The sky had turned yellow and still. Nothing moved in it. No birds, no clouds. You couldn't see the sun. Just a pale yellow sky. Made me feel twitchy in the stomach.

Mr. Cobb got us close to Concord, then followed Pap's directions. Suddenly I recognized a stand of pine. And then the beginning of Doc Winston's fence.

"That's it," I said.

"Good. This storm looks nasty. I don't want to be driving in it someplace I don't know."

Mr. Cobb parked outside the gate. I opened my car door. The hair stood up on my arms. It was still as death outside Doc Winston's house. I heard no barking. Peering through the gate, my eyes searched for signs of Sable.

As I stood there, the sky opened. In a moment my overalls and T-shirt were soaking wet. Rain beat down through my hair and trickled along my scalp.

"Get back in the car, Tate," Mr. Cobb called.

"No, sir!" I cried.

I opened the gate and slipped through, calling for Sable.

Sable didn't come. Maybe Doc Winston had her in the house.

I rang the bell. Doc Winston opened his front door and motioned me inside.

Standing in his front hall, I dripped onto the pale patterned rug.

It took a while for me to explain who I was and what I was doing there.

"You've come looking for the dog?" Doc Winston asked.

"Yes, sir," I said. "Sable."

"Why, she's been gone for weeks," Doc Winston said. "I'm so sorry you didn't call before coming all this way."

"She's gone?" I asked.

Doc Winston nodded. "She just took off one day and never came back."

"Why didn't you tell us?"

"I thought it would just upset you," Doc Winston said. "Besides, your knowing wouldn't have brought her back."

"You lost her!" I cried. "You lost Sable."

"Come into the kitchen, honey," Doc Winston said. "Let me give you something warm to drink."

"No!" I cried. "I mean, no. Thank you, sir. Mr. Cobb's waiting for me out in the car. I have to go."

I looked back at Doc Winston before stepping out into the rain. "If you see her you'll call, won't you?"

Doc Winston nodded.

I stumbled back to Mr. Cobb's car. The water streamed down my neck and my back and filled my shoes. My feet squished as I walked. I couldn't have been wetter if I'd laid down fully dressed in a tub of water.

Mr. Cobb kept the heater running while he took care of his business in Concord.

We had to stop a lot on the way home because of branches down in the road. Mr. Cobb would put on the brake and I'd get out and drag the fallen limbs to the side so we could pass. Some of those branches weighed more than I did, but getting in and out of the car was hard on Mr. Cobb, so I took care of it.

I still hadn't said a word about Sable when our driveway came into view, but I guess Mr. Cobb knew pretty much how things had gone.

"Sorry the day didn't turn out better for you, Tate," Mr. Cobb said.

I just stared at my hands.

10/Cleaning Up

It looked like a tornado had cut across our property. Mam's willow lay in a mess of branches across the front yard. The shed behind Pap's shop sprawled on its side. Mam's clothesline was down. So was one of the power lines.

I ran toward the house, afraid something might have happened to Mam and Pap.

They flew out the kitchen door at the same time, onto the back porch, stopping when they saw me. They kind of leaned into each other at the top of the steps.

Mr. Cobb waited till I reached the porch. Then he tooted his horn once and waved good-bye.

"Glad you're back," Pap said.

I told Mam and Pap about the tree limbs down in the road. I told them about the yellow sky and the silence before the storm broke.

"Did you see Sable?" Pap asked.

"No, sir," I said.

Mam and Pap looked at me, questioning.

"I'd rather not talk about it," I said.

"Well," Pap said, "I've got some cleaning up to do."

"I do, too," said Mam.

I looked across the yard. The fence I'd made for Sable still stood. All but one sticker. I'd built a good fence for Sable. Only there wasn't any Sable to put inside it.

I turned to Mam and Pap. "How can I help?" I asked.

Pap put his hand on my shoulder and steered me toward the clothesline. After we got that restrung, we lifted the shed back on its foundation using the pickup truck and a winch and pulley. Some of the shed's contents had blown around the yard. I gathered up everything still in one piece.

The box that once was Sable's bed sat in a gully, against a rock. The cardboard had collapsed into a soggy mess. There was no saving it.

I started cleaning up willow branches, but Pap made me stay clear of them until the power company fixed the line.

As we walked across the backyard for the last time that day, Pap stooped and picked up the one fence post that had let go.

"You built a good fence, Tate Marshall," Pap said.

"Yes, sir."

"I didn't know you could." Pap looked up toward the mountains.

"No, sir," I said. "I don't believe you did."

"Putting a fence in like that takes a lot of planning, a lot of hard work."

"I did it for Sable, Pap."

"I know, Tate."

Pap handed me the broken fence post. I wrapped my arms around it like it was a baby.

11 / The Arrival Again

🐾 Then one day, in early summer, with the mountains deepening to a thick green, I listened as Pap's saw hummed steadily across the yard. I was rinsing breakfast dishes for Mam, thinking about the project waiting for me over in the shop.

Pap had started teaching me his trade. He kept right on top of me when I used his machines, but he let me try more and more all the time.

Between the dishes and the saw, I didn't hear the chug of a motor until the car had nearly reached the top of our driveway. Dust hovered in the thick air.

"Mam," I called, recognizing the car through the screen door. "Looks like Mr. Cobb's here for you." With me taking over some of Mam's chores around the house, Mam had started balancing Mr. Cobb's books, the way she balanced Pap's.

Mr. Cobb got out slowly and opened the back door of his car. He bent his scrawny legs and lifted something off the car seat.

Standing at the sink, looking over my shoulder, I felt my heart start slamming against my chest.

Eden slid off the porch and hid.

Mr. Cobb was talking real gentle as he set something down in front of him.

Moving a little to the side, he revealed a dog. A dark brown dog.

It can't be Sable, I thought.

The dog swayed for a moment, trying to keep its balance. It stared down at the ground, like its head weighed too much to hold up. But one step at a time it came, limping up the path toward the porch.

"Mam!"

My heart nailed at my throat like it meant to stick there.

"Mam! I think it's Sable."

The screen door banged shut behind me as I flew outside.

I crouched down in front of the dog and held out my hand. The thin brown dog trembled. Her tail, tipped on the end with white, waved once like a tired arm.

"Sable?"

I spoke gently. The dog took a step forward. She lifted her head. But she didn't look straight at me. She had a braided twine collar, tied with a ratty square knot, hanging around her neck.

"Sable? It is you, isn't it, girl!"

She wagged her tail.

Sable looked closer to death than she had the first time she'd wandered into our lives. I could count the ribs in her brown chest and the bones along her spine. Dried blood caked her paws, and she limped pretty bad.

"Tate?" Pap called from the door of his shop. "Tate, what's going on?"

"Pap!" I called back. "Mr. Cobb found Sable!"

Pap's long legs carried him quickly across the yard.

He crouched beside me.

Sable limped between the two of us and rested her muzzle on my arm. Pap's fingers ran through her fur, watching for any sign of pain. Sable lifted her head, sniffing my hair.

"Sable," I whispered.

She turned, and this time she looked straight at me. That same chocolate look, sweet and dark and shining.

"I was heading over the mountain just now when I saw her," Mr. Cobb said. "It's a good thing I wasn't going too fast or I'd have hit her. Limping right down the center of the road, she was."

Mr. Cobb's driving had made me crazy the day

I'd gone with him to Concord. It didn't make me crazy anymore.

"Thank you, Elton," Pap said. "I'm sure Tate's glad to see her again."

"I thought she might be," Mr. Cobb said.

It looked to me like Pap didn't mind seeing her again too much either.

And then the strangest thing happened.

Mam walked over, reached down her hand, and touched Sable.

Sable held so still, like she knew how hard it was, what Mam was doing.

Mam's fingers spread slowly over Sable's head, taking in the bones. Her tall back relaxed a little. She moved her fingertips down, inching toward Sable's ears. Mam smiled as she touched those ears.

"I'll just fetch the first-aid kit," Pap said.

He turned as he went through the back door. "What do you think of that, Tate? Finding her way home, all the way from Concord."

Home! Pap had said home!

I couldn't keep my hands off Sable. I never left her side. Never even waved good-bye to Mr. Cobb.

Doctoring Sable, Pap and I found some ugly sores. Pap cut part of her fur away to dress them.

Mam went in and fried up a mess of hamburg. "For lunch," she said, although it wasn't nearly eleven. Then she didn't even serve any to me or Pap. She just put down a dish for Sable.

Sable had plenty chance to wander off after she came back. She never did.

"I guess you've finally had your fill of wandering, girl," I said, stroking her dark head. "We never even needed that fence."

Sable and I took the fence down. It took a lot less time knocking it apart than it took hammering it together.

Sable never knew I'd built that fence for her. But she sure enjoyed taking it apart. She'd steal a sticker and race around the property with it, then come back and trot beside me, carrying her sticker while

I carted a load of my own, off to the woodshed for winter kindling.

Sable even started coming inside the house. You could tell where she'd been by the trail of sawdust she left. Pap and I had to clean up our tracks with the broom and dustpan. Mam cleaned up after Sable.

At night, Sable curled by the kitchen woodstove, thumping her tail whenever Mam walked by. And once, while Mam was fixing dinner, I swear she handed a good piece of meat down to that dog. And Sable took it from her easy, real easy.

"Mam!" I cried. "What are you doing?"

"It's just a bite, Tate," Mam said.

As if Sable needed a reason for staying.

About the Author and Illustrator

Karen Hesse's own family dog, Sasha, is a black mutt who wandered into their lives in much the same way Sable did.

Ms. Hesse is the author of *Letters from Rifka*, winner of the Christopher Medal, the National Jewish Book Award, an ALA Notable Book, and an ALA Best Book for Young Adults. Her many other books for young readers include *Phoenix Rising*, an ALA Notable Book and an ALA Best Book for Young Adults, *Lavender*, and *Wish on a Unicorn*.

A native of Baltimore, Maryland, Karen Hesse lives with her family in Williamsville, Vermont.

Marcia Sewall is the illustrator of many books for children, including *Nobody's Cat*. She lives in Dorchester, Massachusetts.